Q & RAY

CASE #1
THE MISSING MOLA LISA

TRISHA SPEED SHASKAN

ILLUSTRATED BY STEPHEN SHASKAN

Graphic Universe™ • Minneapolis

For my sister Nicole, for introducing me to so many greats, including Sherlock Holmes, and for her continual support. Love you! —TSS

To my dad, who encouraged me to create art and collect comics —SS

Graphic Universe™
A division of Lerner Publishing Group, Inc.
241 First Avenue North
Minneapolis, MN 55401 USA

For reading levels and more information, look up this title at www.lernerbooks.com.

Main body text set in CCDaveGibbonsLower 11.5/13.25.
Typeface provided by ComicCraft.

Library of Congress Cataloging-in-Publication Data

Names: Shaskan, Trisha Speed, 1973–, author. | Shaskan, Stephen, illustrator.
Title: The missing Mola Lisa: case #1 / Trisha Speed Shaskan ; illustrated by Stephen Shaskan.
Description: Minneapolis : Graphic Universe, [2017] | Summary: "Quillan Hedgeson, a hedgehog, and Raymond Ratzberg, a rat, are students (and crime solvers) at Elm Tree Elementary school. When a theft occurs during a class trip to the local art museum, Q and Ray set out to solve the case, using their wits and a series of disguises" —Provided by publisher.
Identifiers: LCCN 2016009537 (print) | LCCN 2016032607 (ebook) | ISBN 9781512411478 (lb : alk. paper) | ISBN 9781512454147 (pb) | ISBN 9781512430226 (eb pdf)
Subjects: LCSH: Graphic novels. | CYAC: Graphic novels. | Mystery and detective stories. | Hedgehogs—Fiction. | Rats—Fiction.
Classification: LCC PZ7.7.S455 Cas 2017 (print) | LCC PZ7.7.S455 (ebook) | DDC 741.5/973—dc23

LC record available at https://lccn.loc.gov/2016009537

Manufactured in the United States of America
1-39653-21285-10/25/2016

WHO'S WHO

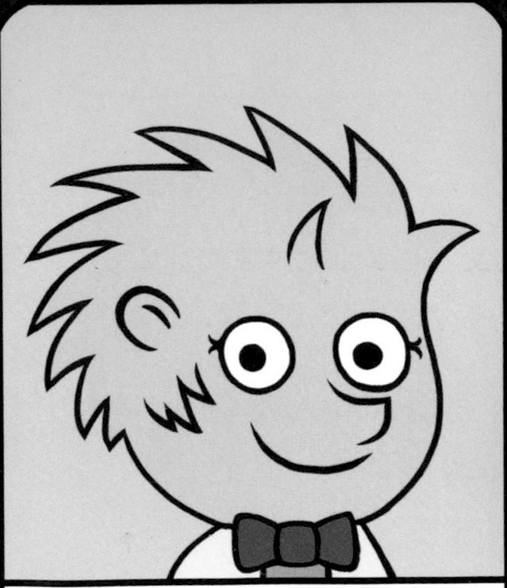

Quillan Lu Hedgeson
aka: Q

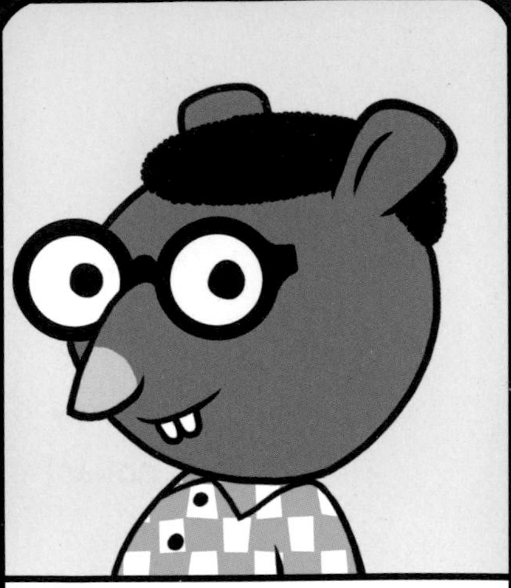

Ray Ratzberg

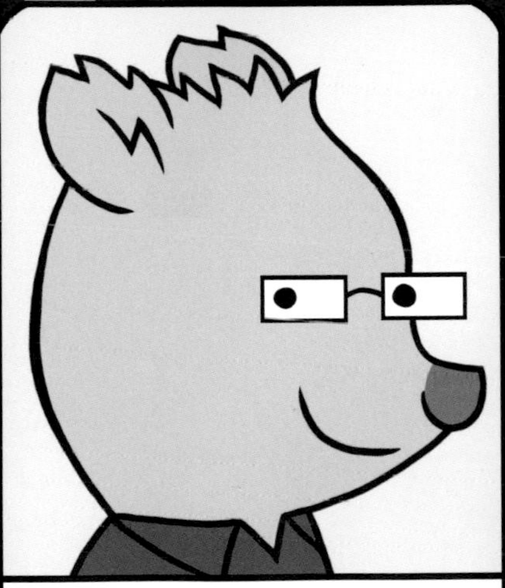

Mr. Shrew
Media Specialist

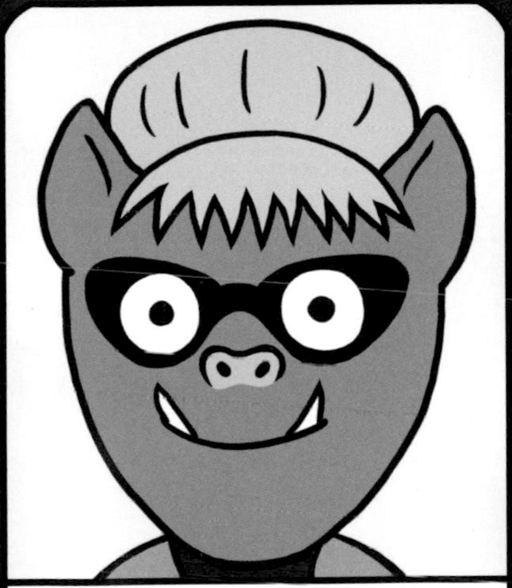

Ms. Boar
Classroom Teacher

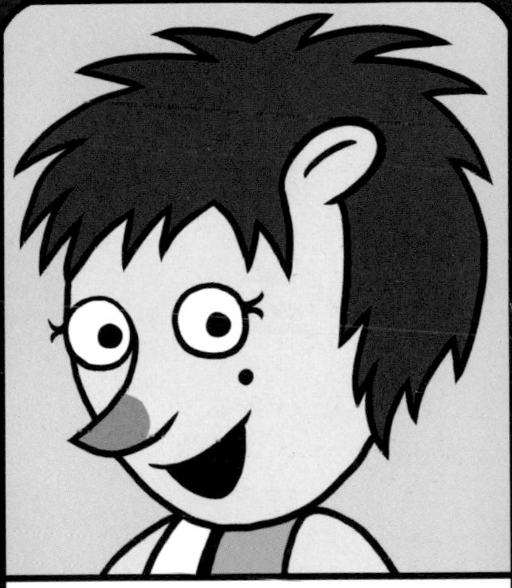

Ms. Easel
Art Teacher

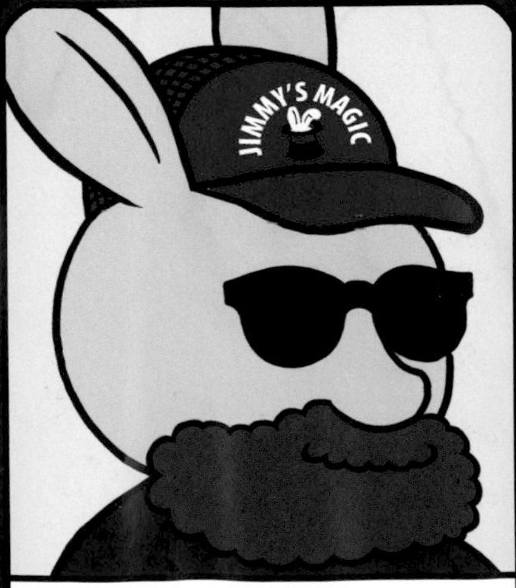
JIMMY'S MAGIC

Jimmy
Magic Shop Owner

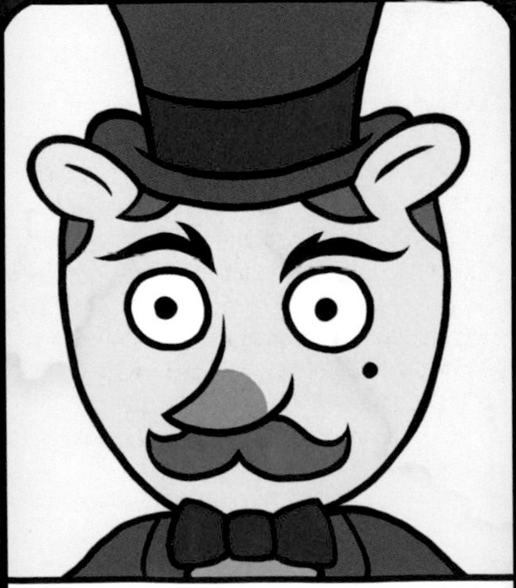

The Great Don Realo
Magician

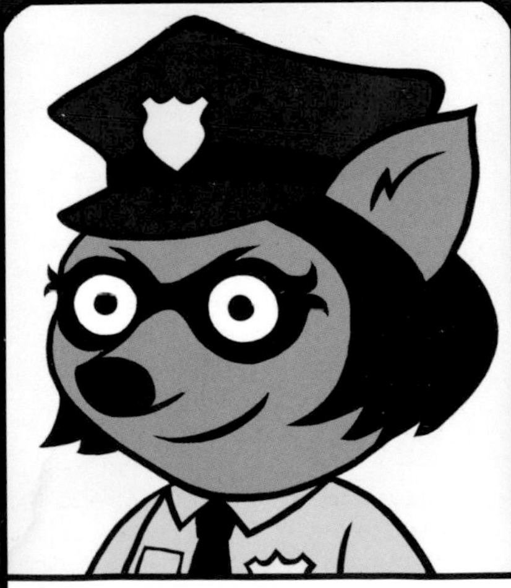

Officer Rocco

CHAPTER ONE
Q and Ray

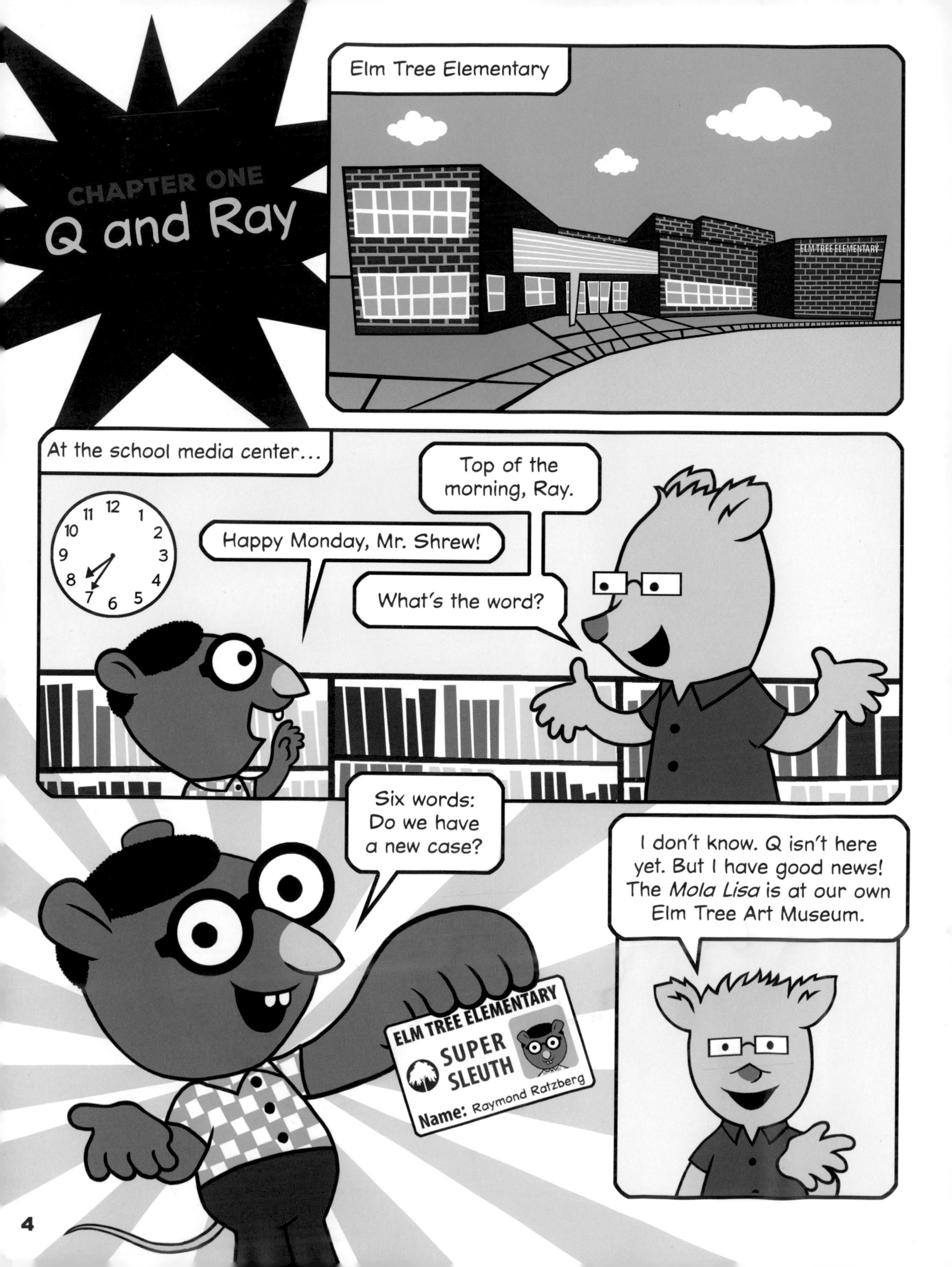

Elm Tree Elementary
ELM TREE ELEMENTARY
At the school media center...
Happy Monday, Mr. Shrew!
Top of the morning, Ray.
What's the word?
Six words: Do we have a new case?
ELM TREE ELEMENTARY
SUPER SLEUTH
Name: Raymond Ratzberg
I don't know. Q isn't here yet. But I have good news! The *Mola Lisa* is at our own Elm Tree Art Museum.

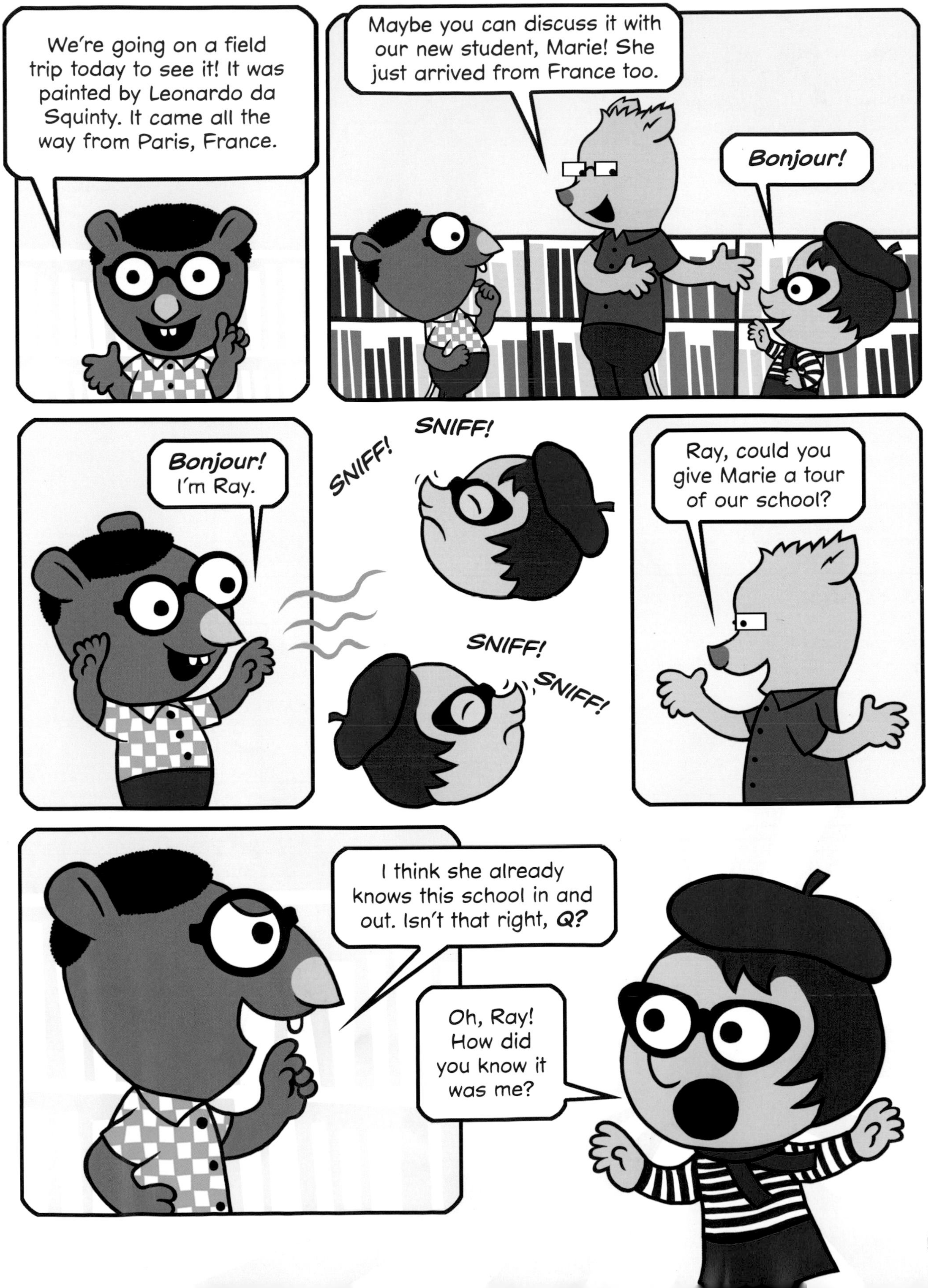
We're going on a field trip today to see it! It was painted by Leonardo da Squinty. It came all the way from Paris, France.
Maybe you can discuss it with our new student, Marie! She just arrived from France too.
Bonjour!
Bonjour! I'm Ray.
SNIFF!
SNIFF!
SNIFF!
SNIFF!
Ray, could you give Marie a tour of our school?
I think she already knows this school in and out. Isn't that right, Q?
Oh, Ray! How did you know it was me?

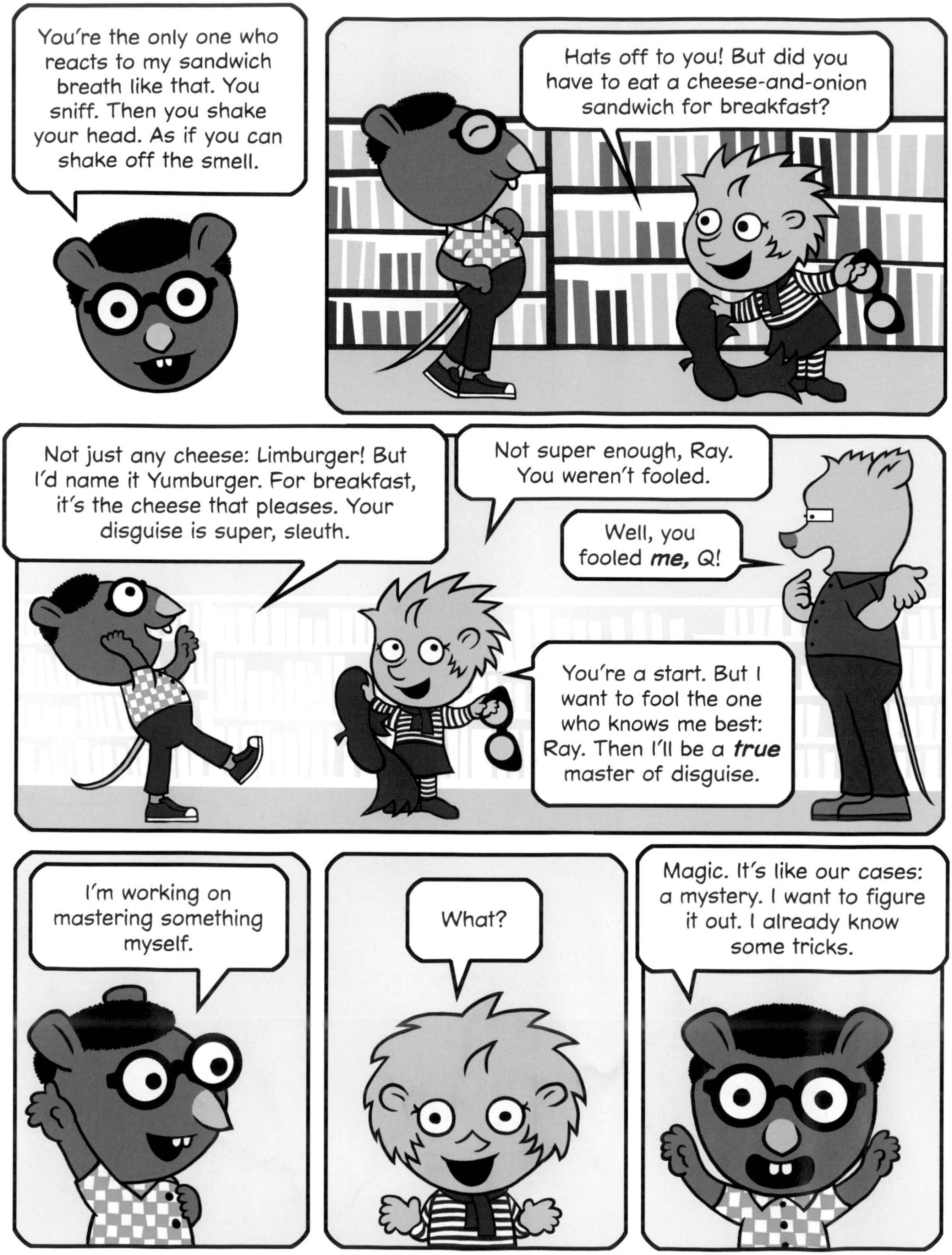
You're the only one who reacts to my sandwich breath like that. You sniff. Then you shake your head. As if you can shake off the smell.
Hats off to you! But did you have to eat a cheese-and-onion sandwich for breakfast?
Not just any cheese: Limburger! But I'd name it Yumburger. For breakfast, it's the cheese that pleases. Your disguise is super, sleuth.
Not super enough, Ray. You weren't fooled.
Well, you fooled *me,* Q!
You're a start. But I want to fool the one who knows me best: Ray. Then I'll be a *true* master of disguise.
I'm working on mastering something myself.
What?
Magic. It's like our cases: a mystery. I want to figure it out. I already know some tricks.

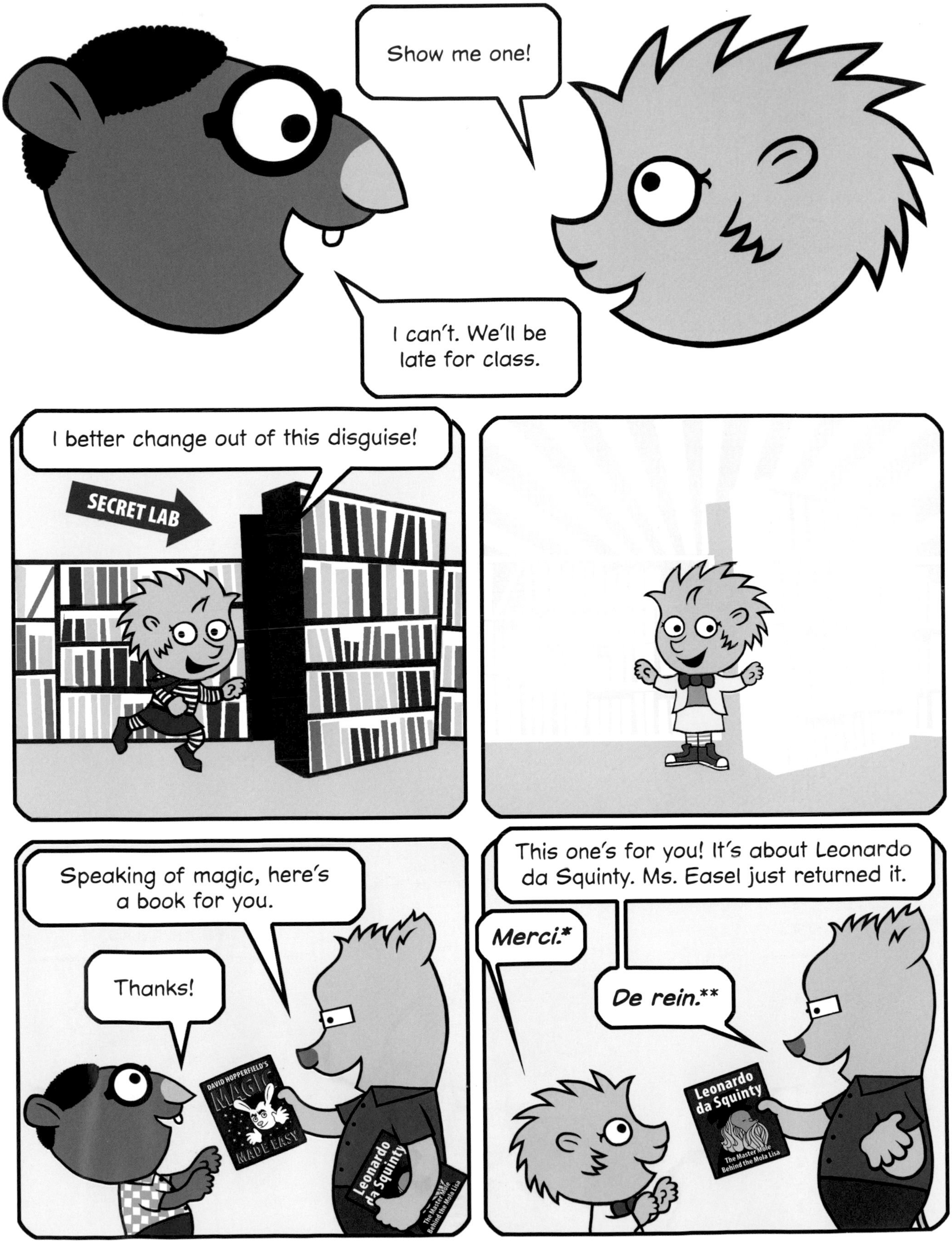
Show me one!
I can't. We'll be late for class.
I better change out of this disguise!
SECRET LAB
Speaking of magic, here's a book for you.
Thanks!
DAVID HOPPERFIELD'S MAGIC MADE EASY
Leonardo da Squinty The Master Mole Behind the Mola Lisa
This one's for you! It's about Leonardo da Squinty. Ms. Easel just returned it.
Merci.*
De rein.**
Leonardo da Squinty The Master Mole Behind the Mola Lisa

*mair-SEE. That's "thank you" in French!
**duh-ree-ehn. That's "you're welcome"!

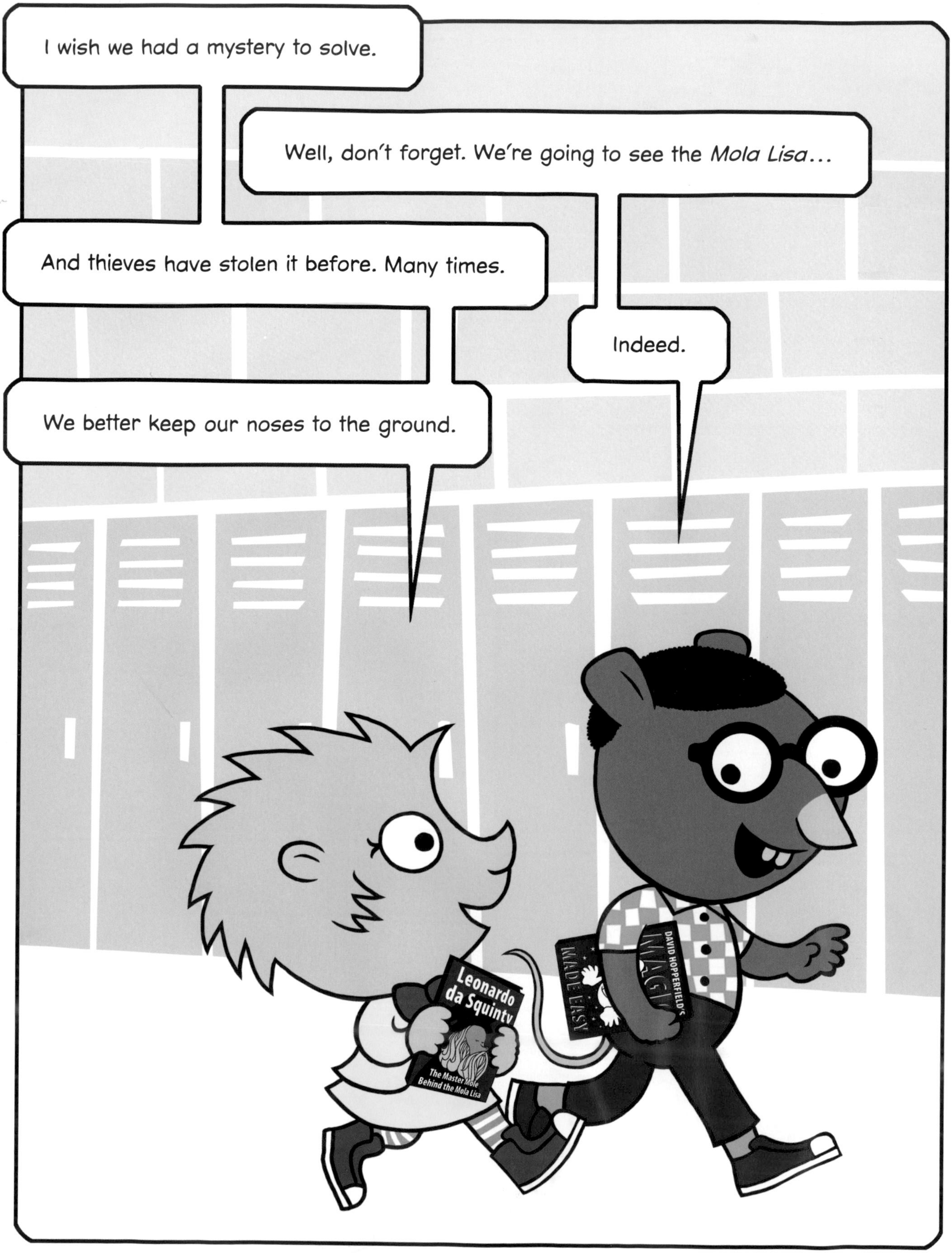
I wish we had a mystery to solve.
Well, don't forget. We're going to see the *Mola Lisa*...
And thieves have stolen it before. Many times.
Indeed.
We better keep our noses to the ground.
Leonardo da Squinty
The Master Mole Behind the Mola Lisa
DAVID HOPPERFIELD'S MAGIC MADE EASY

CHAPTER TWO
The Magic Show

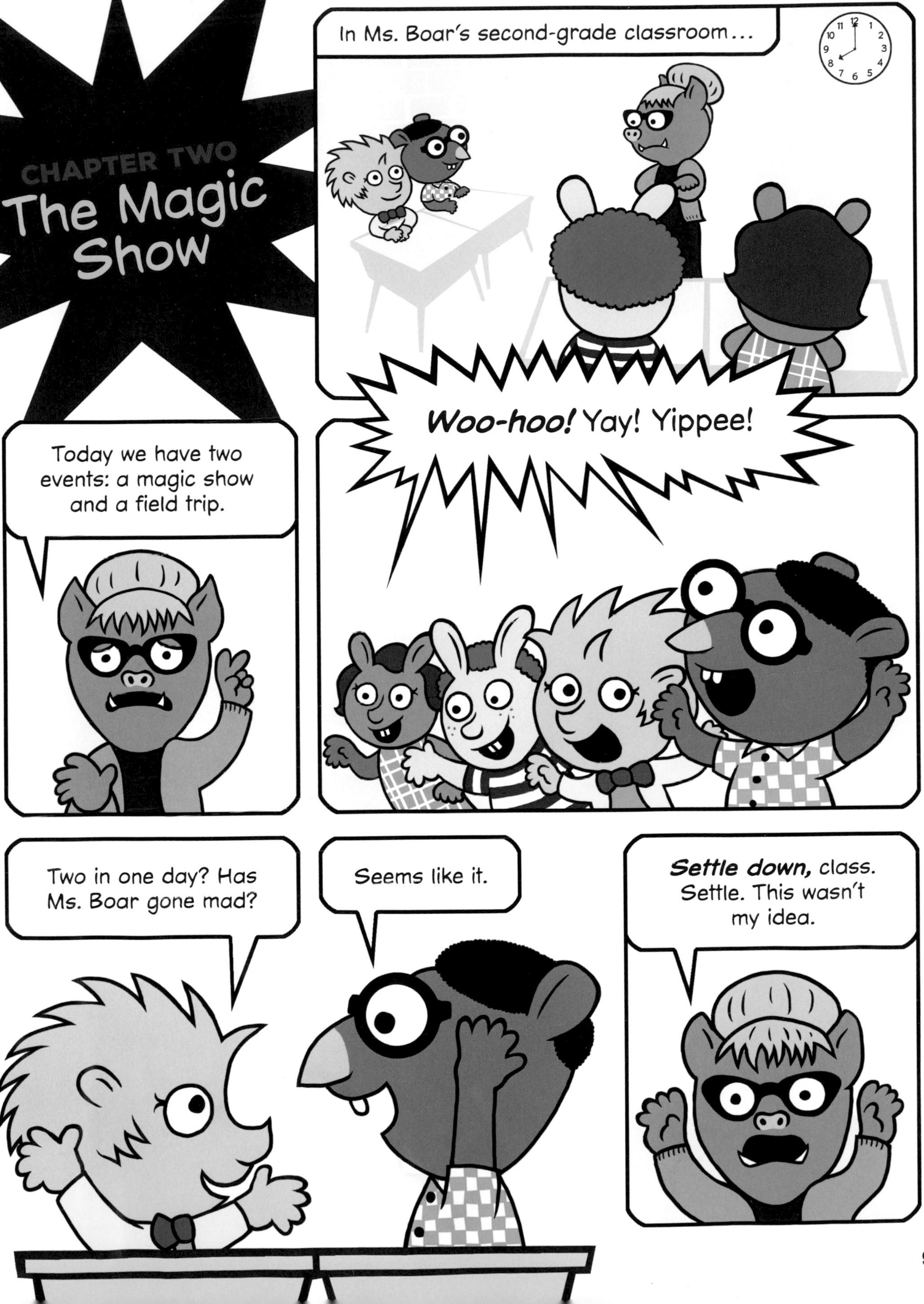
In Ms. Boar's second-grade classroom...
Today we have two events: a magic show and a field trip.
Woo-hoo! Yay! Yippee!
Two in one day? Has Ms. Boar gone mad?
Seems like it.
Settle down, class. Settle. This wasn't my idea.

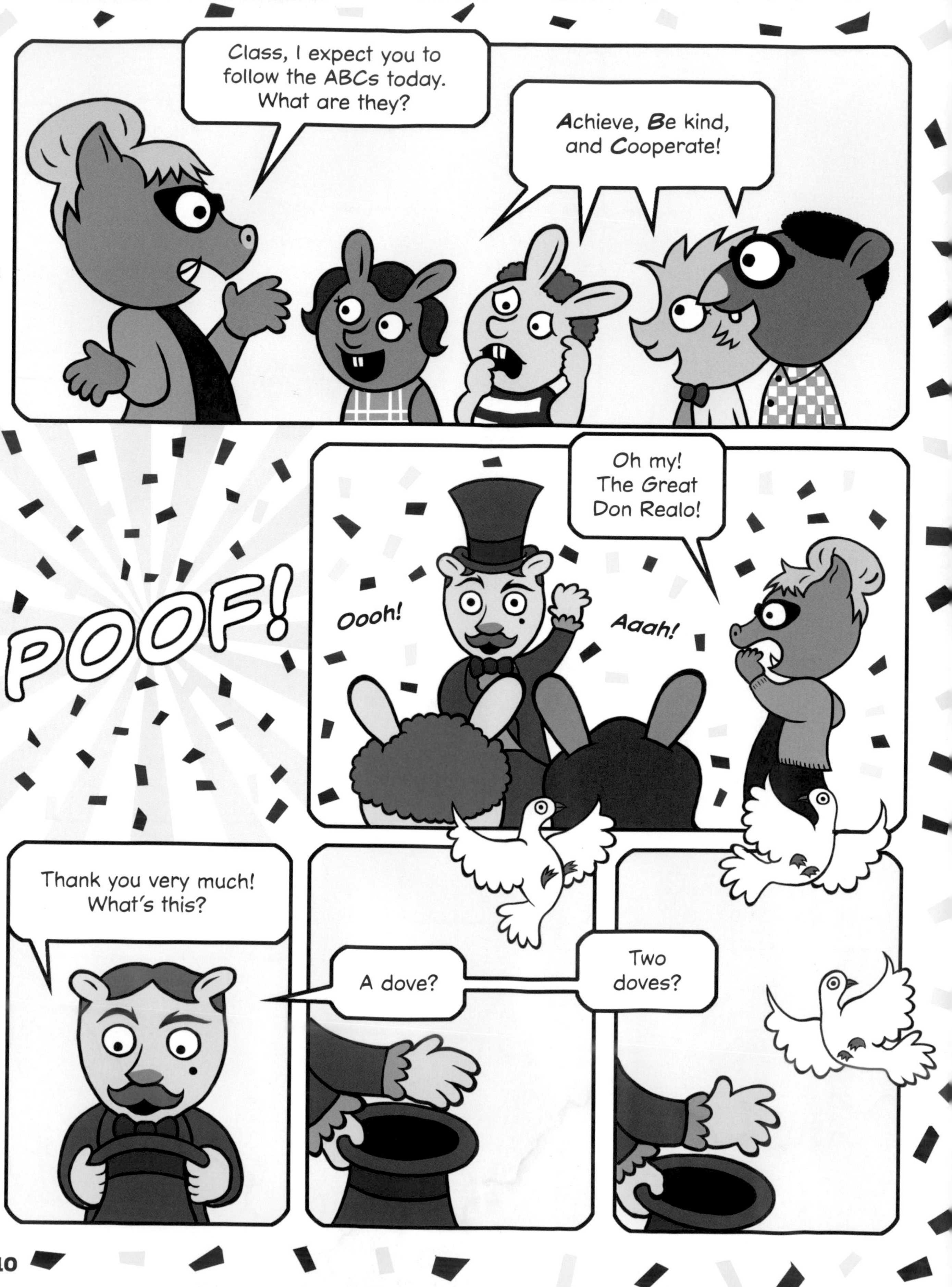
Class, I expect you to follow the ABCs today. What are they?
Achieve, Be kind, and Cooperate!
POOF!
Oooh!
Aaah!
Oh my! The Great Don Realo!
Thank you very much! What's this?
A dove?
Two doves?

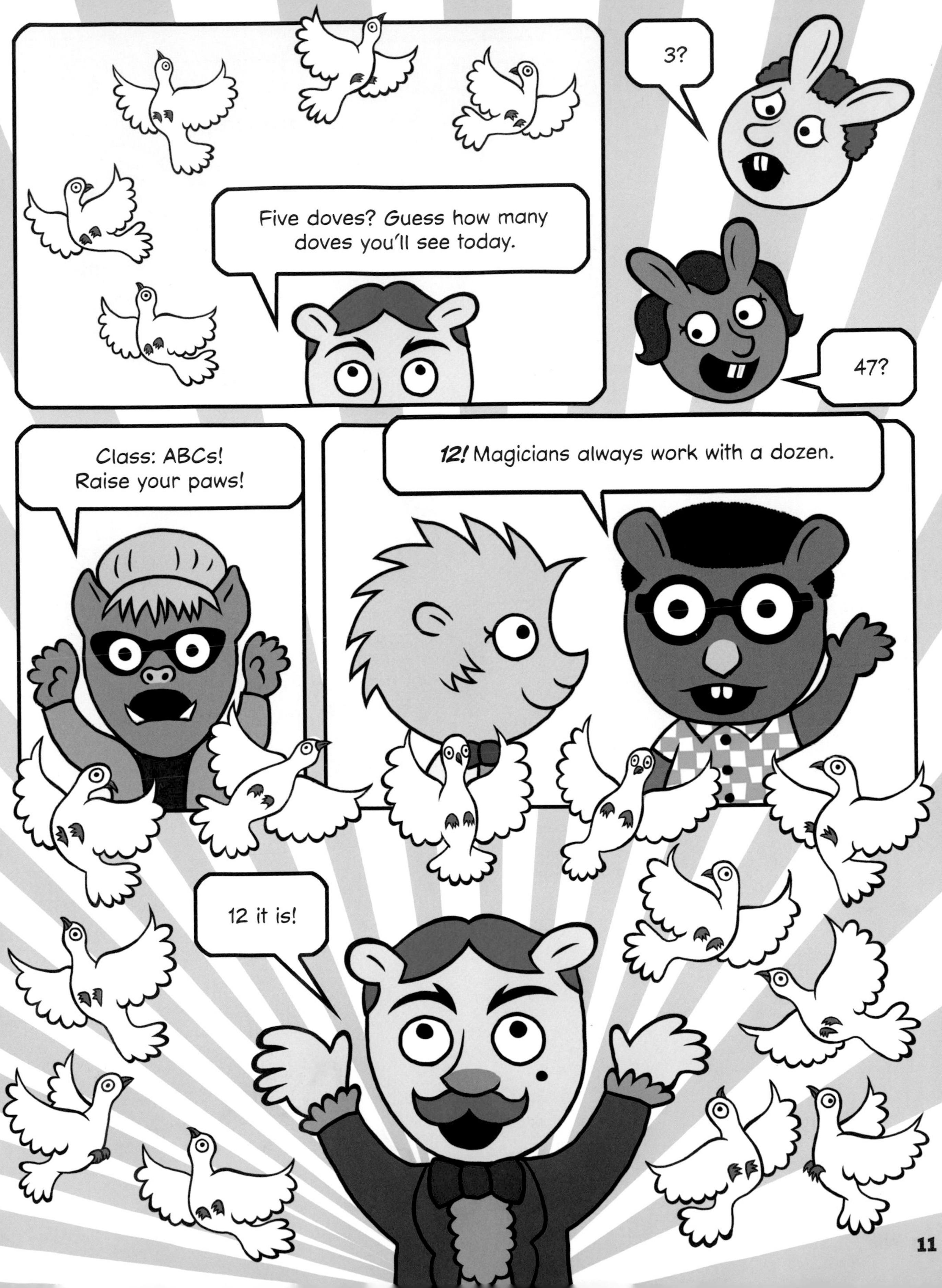
Five doves? Guess how many doves you'll see today.
3?
47?
Class: ABCs! Raise your paws!
12! Magicians always work with a dozen.
12 it is!

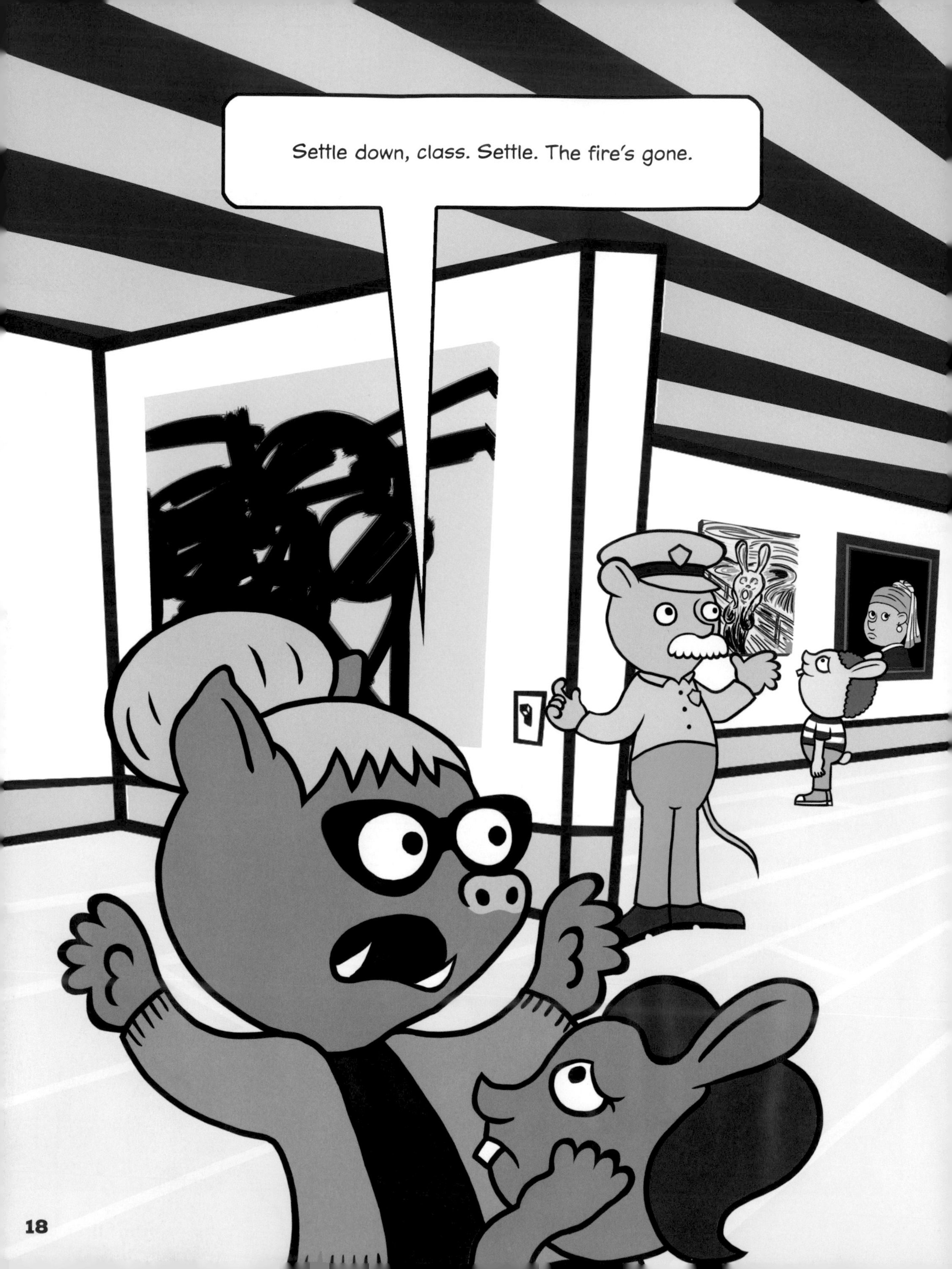
Settle down, class. Settle. The fire's gone.

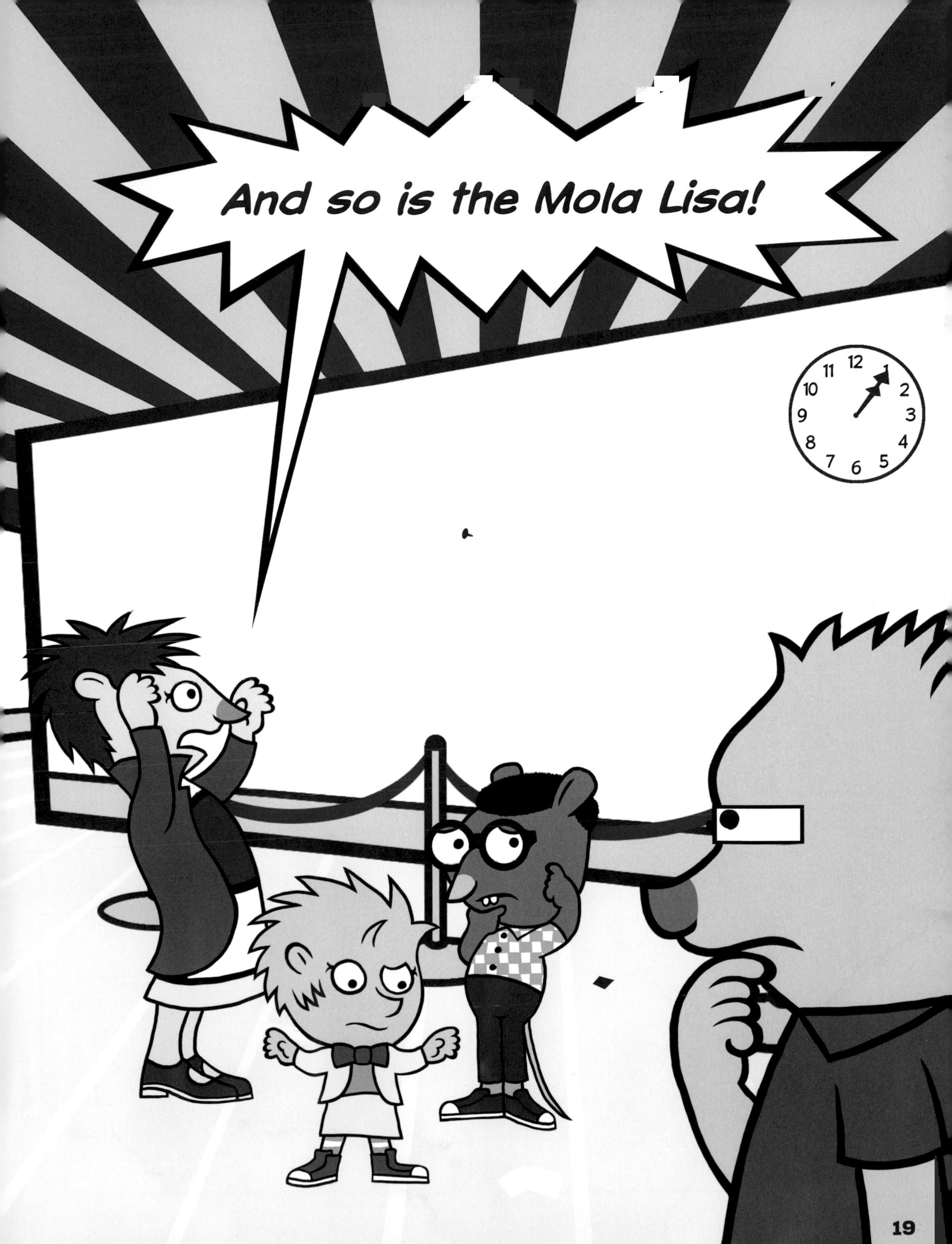
And so is the Mola Lisa!

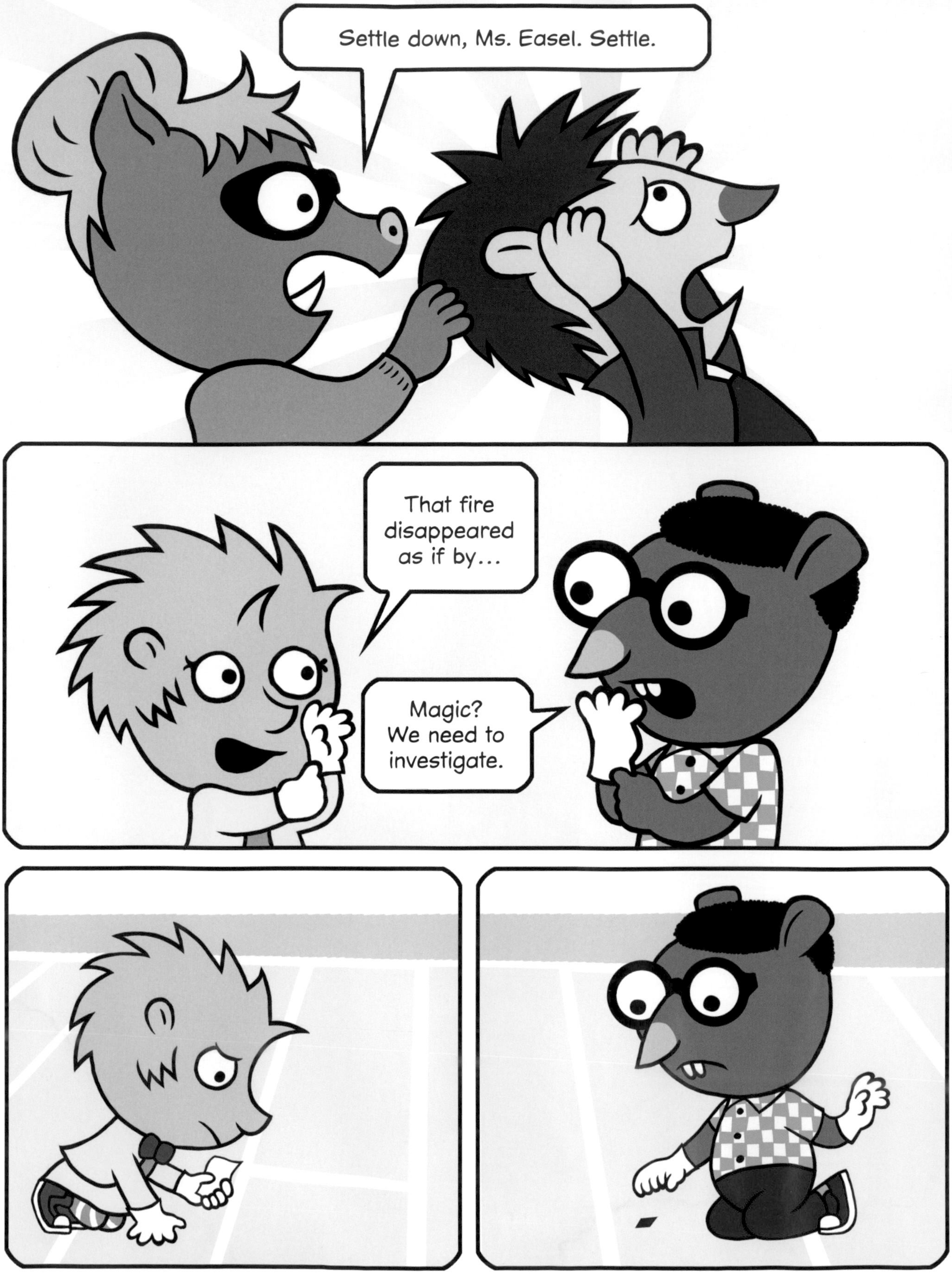

Settle down, Ms. Easel. Settle.
That fire disappeared as if by...
Magic? We need to investigate.

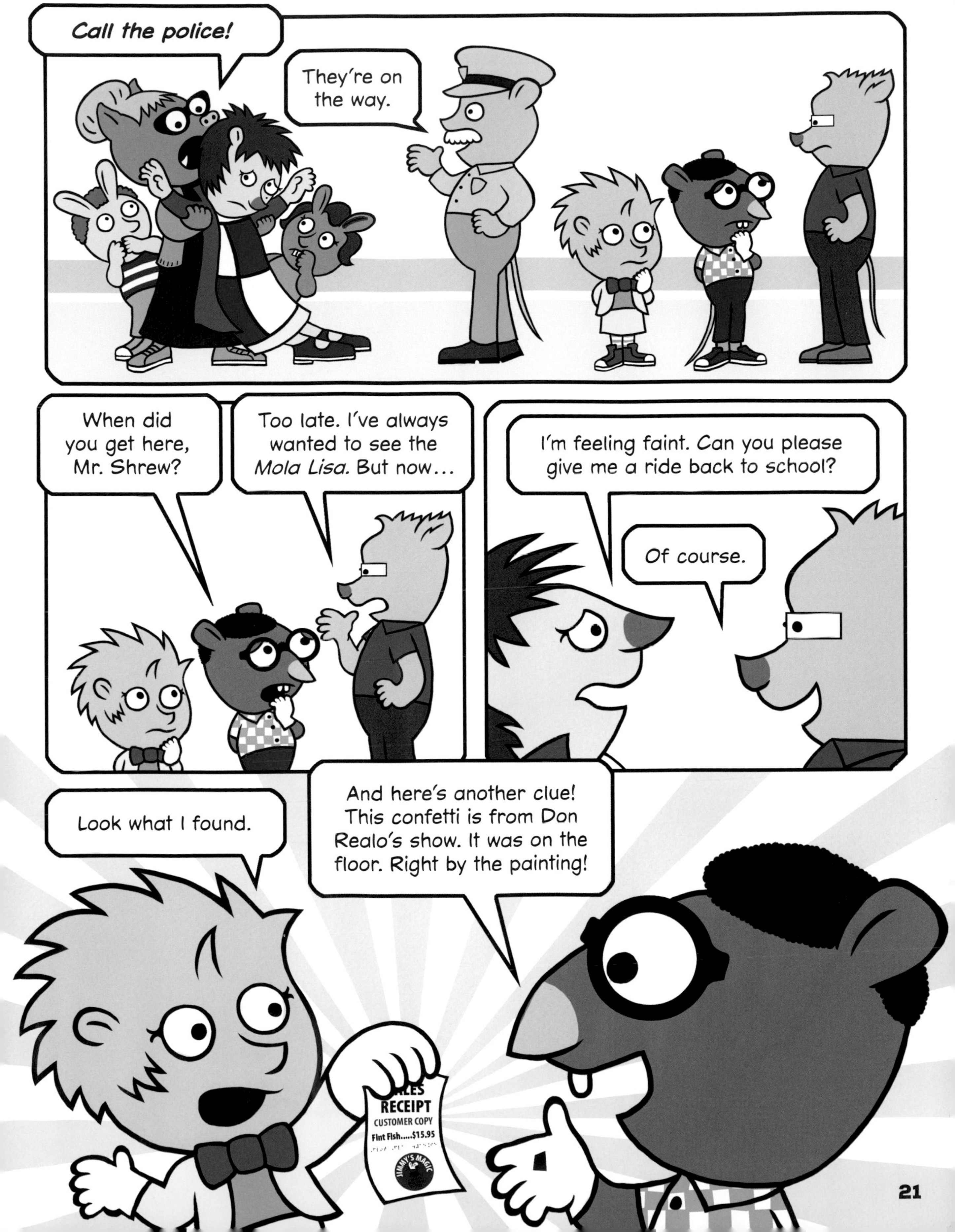

Call the police!
They're on the way.
When did you get here, Mr. Shrew?
Too late. I've always wanted to see the *Mola Lisa.* But now…
I'm feeling faint. Can you please give me a ride back to school?
Of course.
Look what I found.
And here's another clue! This confetti is from Don Realo's show. It was on the floor. Right by the painting!
RECEIPT
CUSTOMER COPY
Flnt Fish.....$15.95
JIMMY'S MAGIC

Searching for Suspects

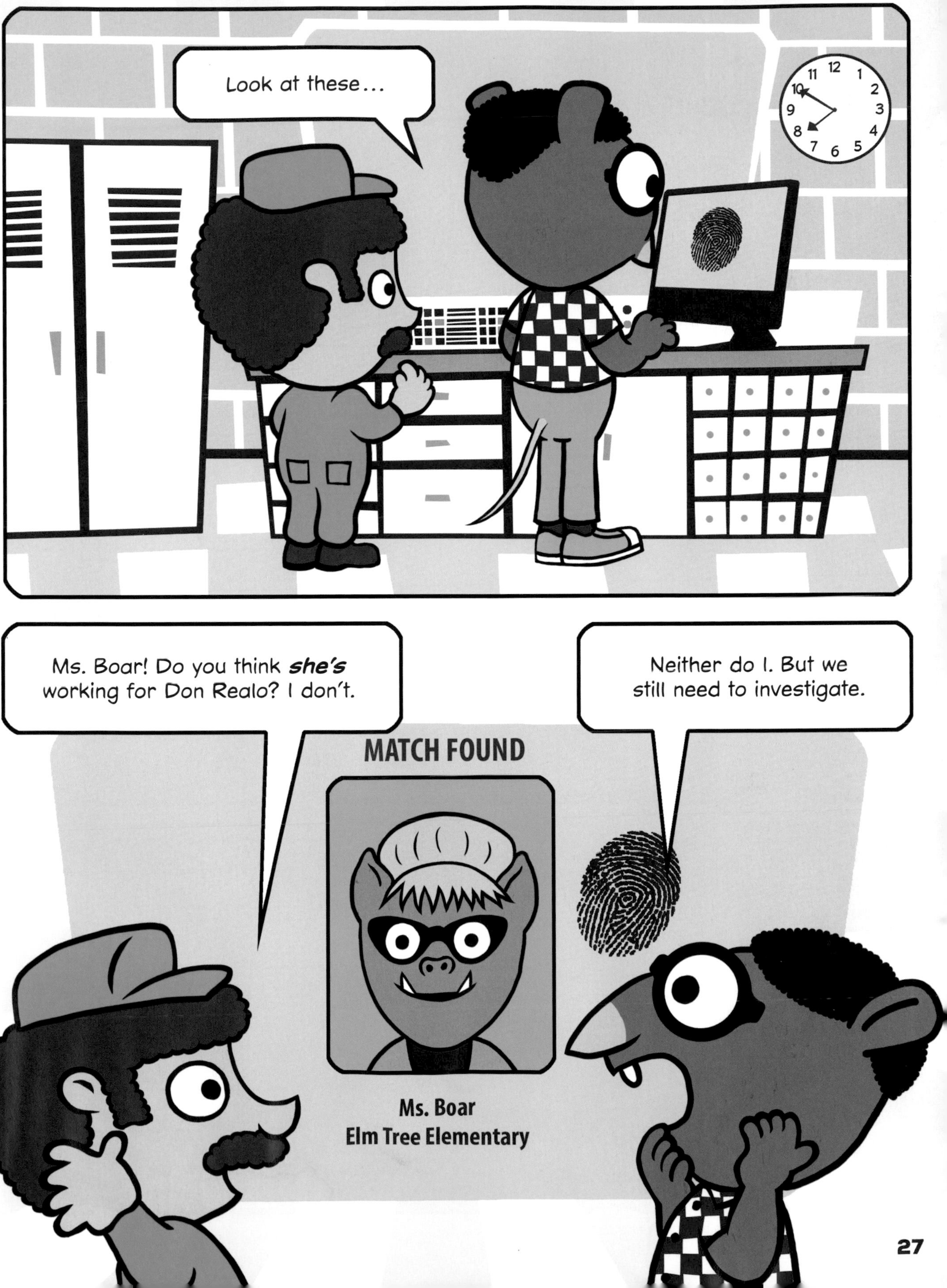
Look at these...
Ms. Boar! Do you think *she's* working for Don Realo? I don't.
Neither do I. But we still need to investigate.
MATCH FOUND
Ms. Boar
Elm Tree Elementary

CHAPTER SEVEN

The Great Don Revealo

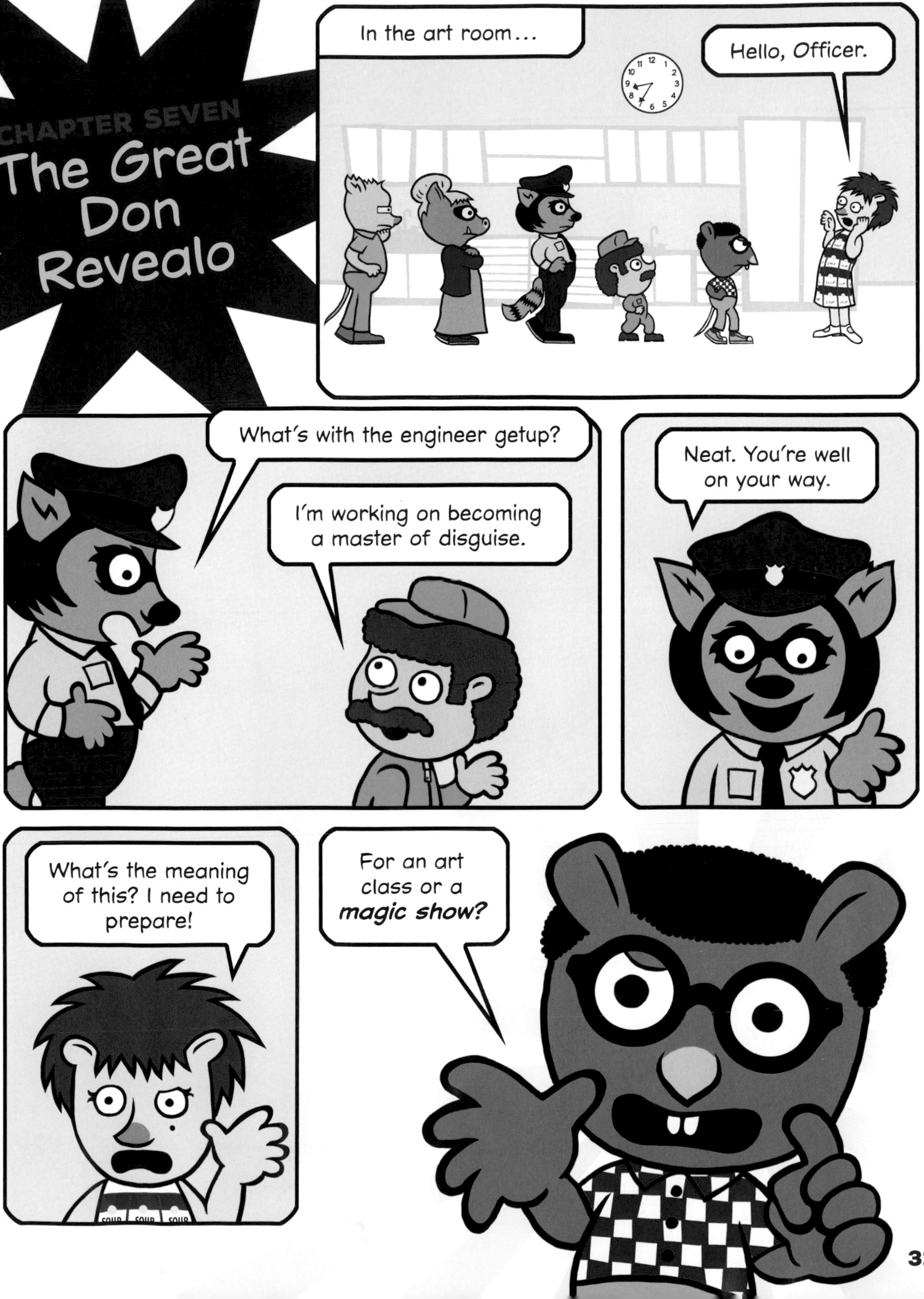

In the art room...
Hello, Officer.
What's with the engineer getup?
I'm working on becoming a master of disguise.
Neat. You're well on your way.
What's the meaning of this? I need to prepare!
For an art class or a *magic show?*
SOUP SOUP SOUP

How did you know Ms. Easel was the Great Don Realo?

I created some images in the lab.

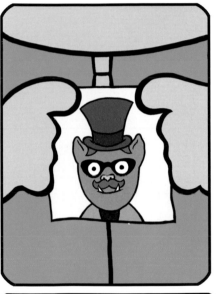

There's no law against dressing like a magician. But do you have proof she stole the painting?

Yesterday, the Great Don Realo performed a magic show for our class. And the painting thief was a true magician!

The lights went out at the art museum. Someone lit a flame. Someone yelled, "Fire." But it was a trick.

CHAPTER EIGHT

More Magic

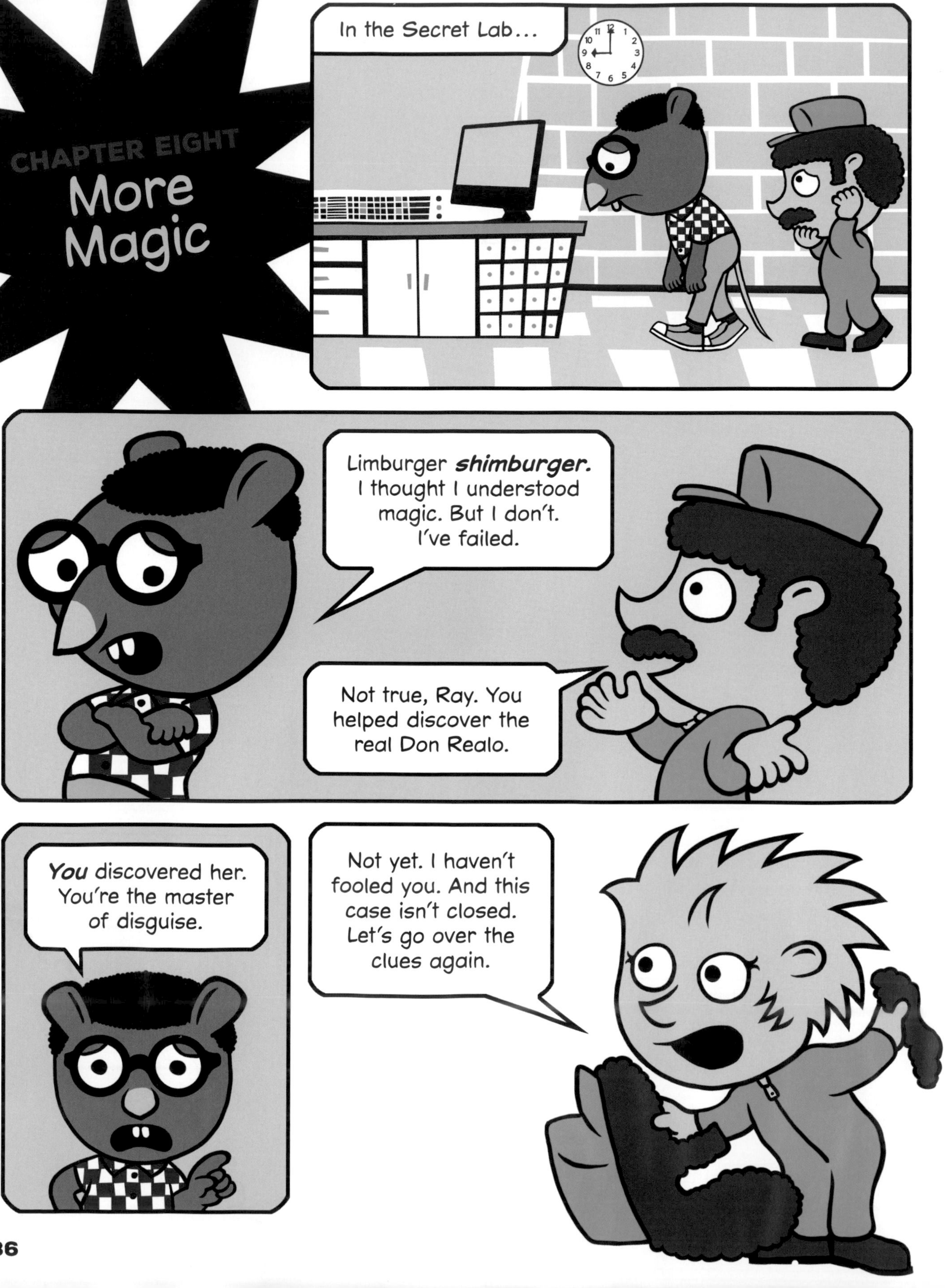
In the Secret Lab...
Limburger ***shimburger.*** I thought I understood magic. But I don't. I've failed.
Not true, Ray. You helped discover the real Don Realo.
You discovered her. You're the master of disguise.
Not yet. I haven't fooled you. And this case isn't closed. Let's go over the clues again.

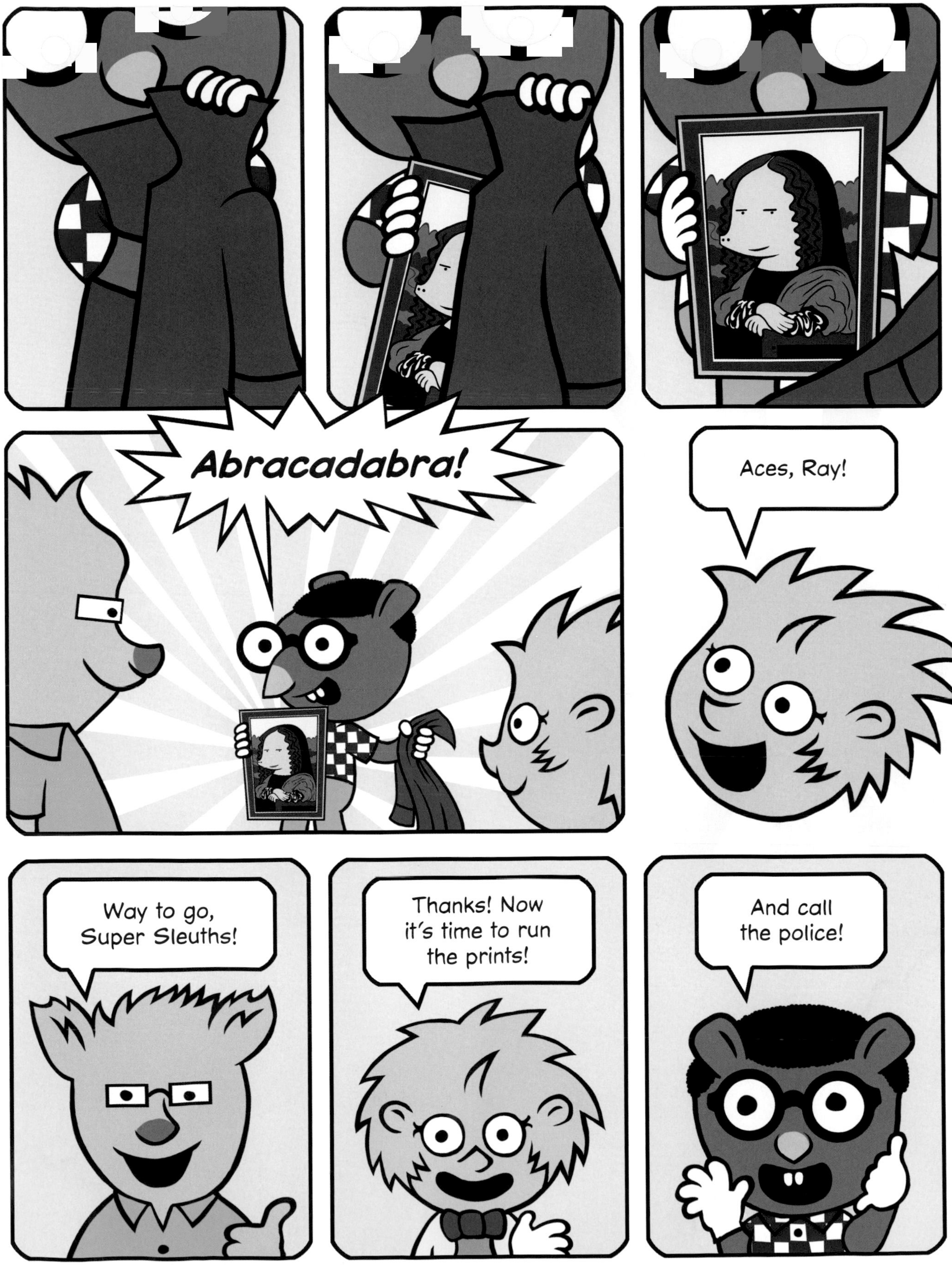
Abracadabra!
Aces, Ray!
Way to go, Super Sleuths!
Thanks! Now it's time to run the prints!
And call the police!

CHAPTER NINE
Evidence!

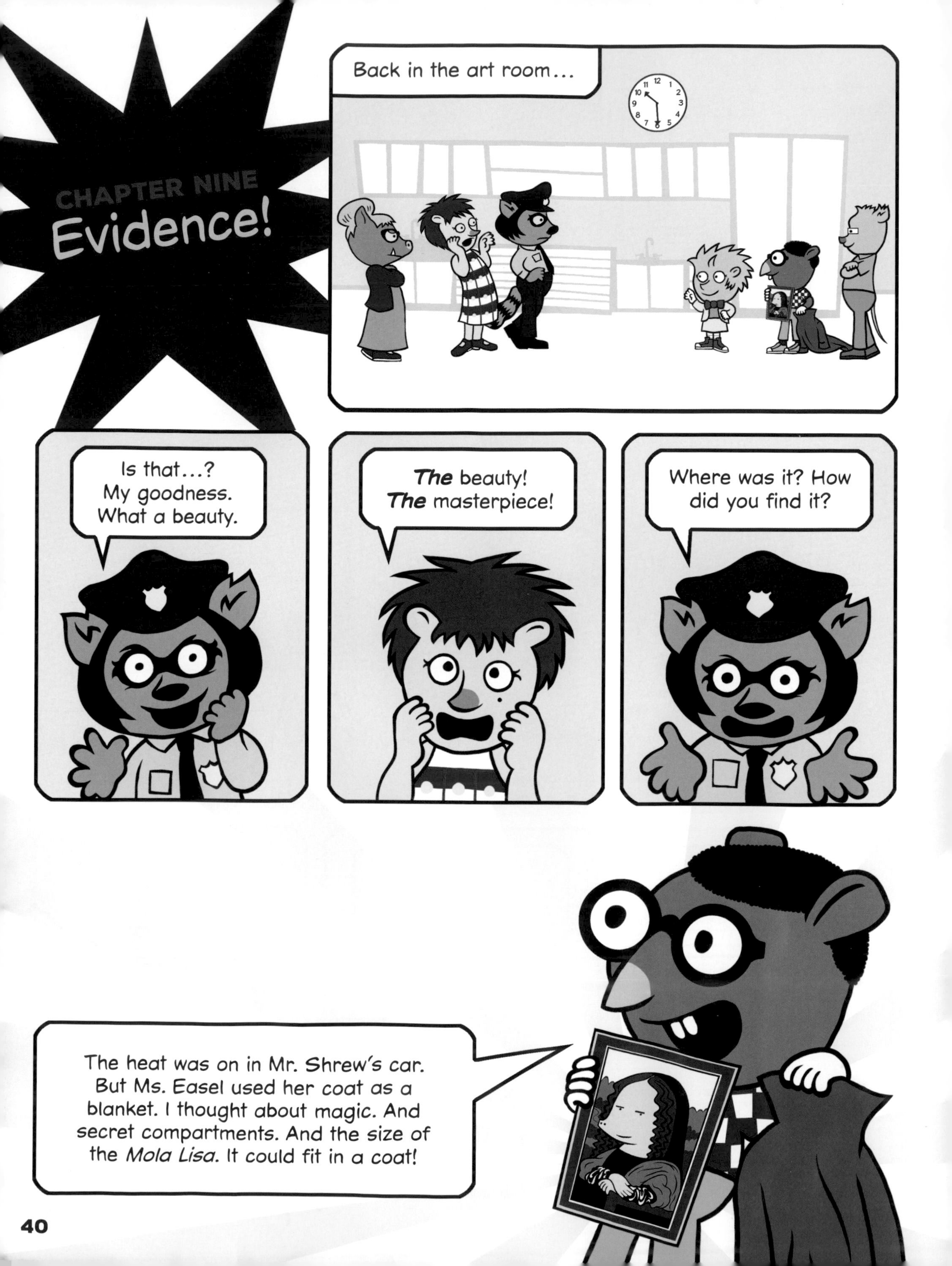
Back in the art room...
Is that...? My goodness. What a beauty.
The beauty! *The* masterpiece!
Where was it? How did you find it?
The heat was on in Mr. Shrew's car. But Ms. Easel used her coat as a blanket. I thought about magic. And secret compartments. And the size of the *Mola Lisa*. It could fit in a coat!

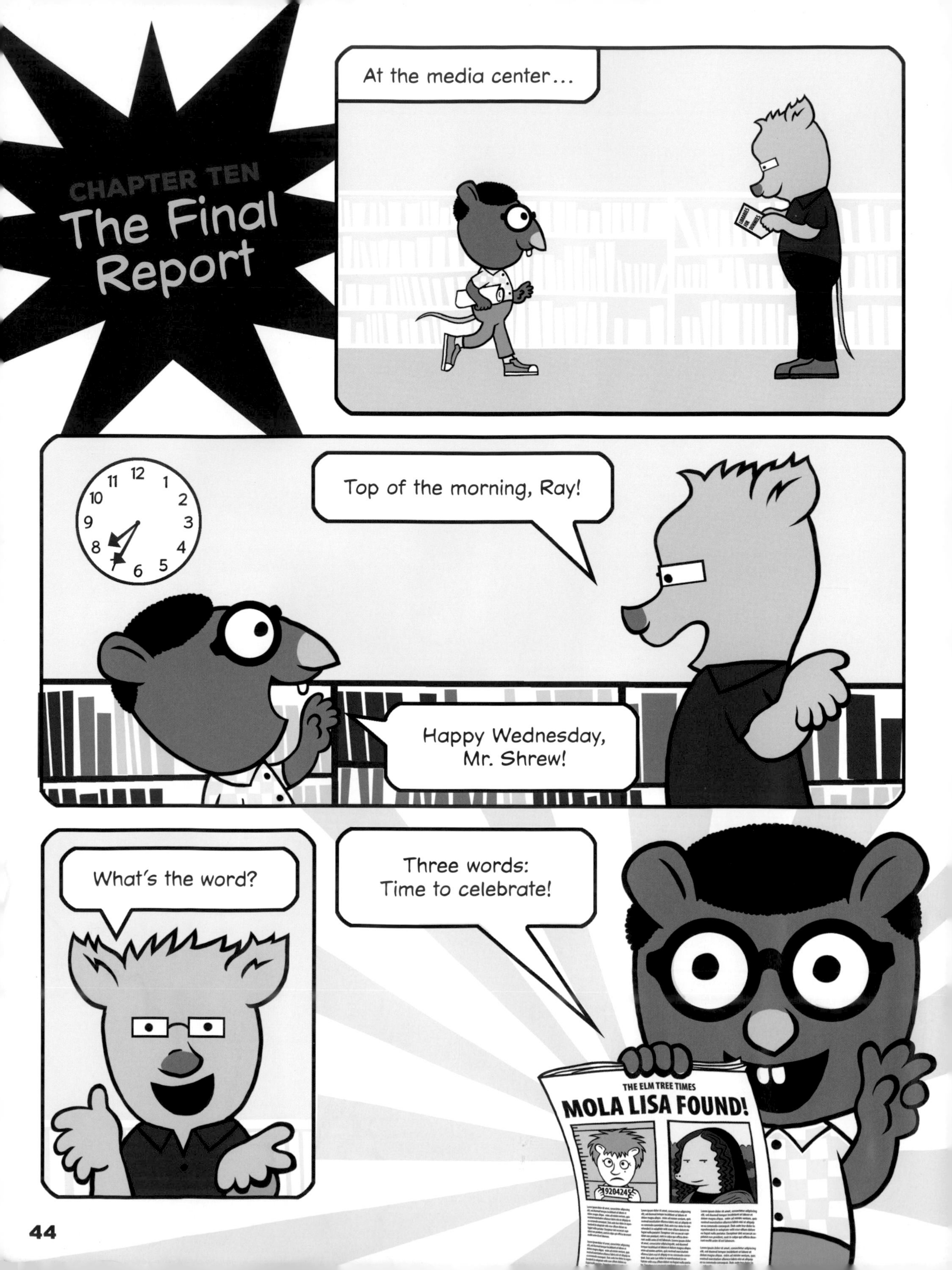
CHAPTER TEN
The Final Report
At the media center...
Top of the morning, Ray!
Happy Wednesday, Mr. Shrew!
What's the word?
Three words: Time to celebrate!
THE ELM TREE TIMES
MOLA LISA FOUND!
9204245

THE END

ABOUT THE AUTHOR

Trisha Speed Shaskan has written more than forty books for children, including her latest picture book, *Punk Skunks*, illustrated by her husband Stephen Shaskan. She received her MFA in creative writing from Minnesota State University, Mankato. She has taught creative writing to students at every level from kindergarten to graduate school. She is super excited to have written her first graphic novel because one of her childhood heroes was—and still is—Wonder Woman. The couple live in Minneapolis, Minnesota, with their dog, Bea, and their cat, Eartha, named after Eartha Kitt, famous for her role as Catwoman.

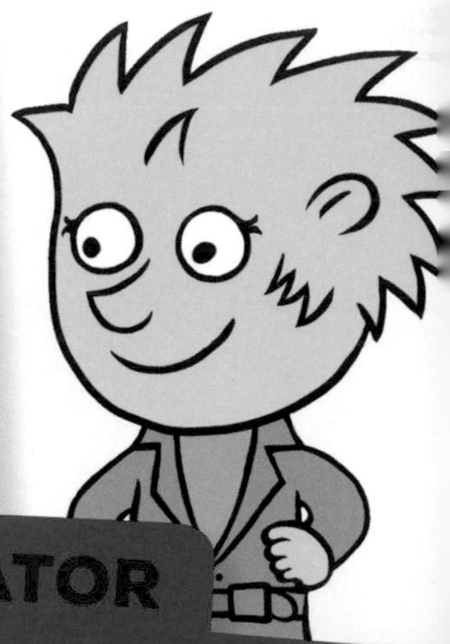

ABOUT THE ILLUSTRATOR

Stephen Shaskan is the author and illustrator of *A Dog Is a Dog*, *Max Speed*, *The Three Triceratops Tuff*, and *Toad on the Road: A Cautionary Tale*. He's the illustrator of *Punk Skunks* too, a book written by his wife, Trisha Speed Shaskan. He's also a graduate of the Rhode Island School of Design, an early childhood educator, and a music maker. And he is super excited to be creating his first graphic novel, since he grew up collecting comic books in upstate New York. He lives in Minneapolis, Minnesota, with his wife, Trisha Speed Shaskan, their cat, Eartha, and their dog, Bea. Visit him at stephenshaskan.com.

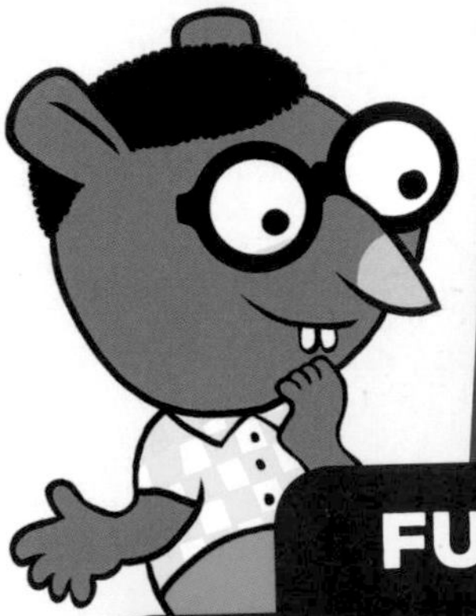

FUN FACTS

LEONARDO DA VINCI

Leonardo da Squinty is based on ***Leonardo da Vinci.***

Leonardo da Vinci was born in 1452 in Italy. Growing up, da Vinci only learned basic reading, writing, and math. But he was a talented artist. His father had him study under a noted sculptor and painter for ten years. At twenty-six years old, da Vinci became a master himself. Four years later, he moved to Milan, Italy. He worked as an engineer and painter. He was also an architect and designer of court festivals.

He lived during a period called the Renaissance (1300–1600). It was a time of great learning in Europe. Many people explored art, science, and literature. Leonardo da Vinci's ideas were way ahead of his time. He made designs that looked like a modern hang glider, a helicopter, and a bicycle.

He was always curious. He wondered why light came from the moon. He wondered why the sky was blue. He used art to explore his questions. His most famous "experiment" is the *Mona Lisa*. It became the most famous painting in the world. And it inspired the *Mola Lisa* too!